...AND ON THE 7TH DAY,

She Rests...

Elizabeth Hope Brown

featuring

Browncommacori

Dedications

This book is dedicated to my three charms, my joys, and my wind beneath, above, beside and all around my wings, Christopher, Elijah, and Cori. Each of you have brought out the best of me, that I would not have seen, had you not been born. Thank you for pushing me to be me, while letting me see you grow your own wings.

To my Mom. For as many words as I know, there never seem to be enough to describe my love, gratitude, and appreciation for your continuous, unconditional love.

In loving memory of my Grandma Lizzie. She asked me to write her story. In many ways, I already have.

Acknowledgement

All Glory Belongs to God.

I'm so thankful that He has blessed me with a village of persons that have undergirded my tenacity to raise my kids the way that He would have them to go. Each of you have given me encouragement and support in your own way. Thank you for allowing me to prioritize myself without guilt and/or explanation.

To my favorite daughter, my one and only Princess, Cori! Thank you for sharing your gifts with me. You have so many talents that I guarantee will not be buried.

To my six sisters that are always candid in love.

To my Sista friends, sister in laws, my children's God parents, and girl cousins that are more like sisters. You've been my ride or die true day ones. We're all in this stew pot together stirring up our gifts.

To my sisters in Christ. Thank you for praying for and with me, when I didn't feel like praying for myself. We all need an entourage on this journey called life.

To my prayer partner. I said I was going to write a book. One day she shook my hand and left a USB flash drive 2-pack in it.

A very special thank you to the Ladies and followers of Lyzee's Hope. This is for all of us "Daring to be all that God has called, designed, and created us to be!"

Finally to everyone reading this book, thank you for sacrificing your time. I pray it is received in the manner in which it is intended.

Foreword

Knowing that this Christian journey is a process, it is important to realize, as the author points out, that the journey takes twists and turns through the secular world. It is also important to know that because of the faith we have or come into and God's promises; we can overcome all obstacles we face on that journey.

I have known Elizabeth Hope Brown for well over ten years as a pastor's wife and friend. She has been exact in all that she does from the sports mom to the social worker to the pastor's wife to being a friend.

In this novel, Elizabeth has used her creative mind to share scenarios of life that we, as women, have found ourselves uniquely caught up and wrapped in on a daily basis. She has addressed the issues presented with biblical insight.

God has given Elizabeth the ability to make His word plain enough for the churched and the unchurched alike to read and see themselves and their situations through the eyes of the characters she presents in this novel. Seven is known as the number of completion. This novel has...seven characters...seven chapters...seven summaries!

As you read through the pages here, you will find yourself and the strength to move to the next level of living in your circumstances for a better life.

Beverly M. Davis, author of "A Spiritual Walk With God", Realtor, National Director 5 Linx Enterprises

Endorsements, Reflections from Family and friends

"I think it's good that my mom did something that she wanted to do. I'm happy she's using the knowledge she has gained from personal experience to teach others."

Christopher, Son, College Senior

"Knowing the author personally, and situations she's been in, or could've been in, I feel as if the book will be appealing to many women."

Elijah, Son, High School Senior

"Proud of my mother for implementing something she really cares about and mixing it with something she loves doing."

Cori, Daughter, High School Freshman

"It is 1978, Teddy Pendergrass sings; "Life is a Song Worth Singing." Elizabeth, 7th Day is a novel worth writing. This is life! Thank You for Part One. MOM"

Christine King-Broomfield, Mom, RN HPMIII, Long Term Care Division, Chief In Home Operations Branch

"I dare any woman to read this and not find pieces of herself. To not want to console or cheer or hug these women. Keep on writing Elizabeth. I want to know what happens next!!! Thanks"

Debbie, Neighbor and Friend of 10+ years

"Elizabeth Brown has written a book to break the silence for woman from all walks of life. This book gets deep into the underlying issues that many women face and are afraid to speak about. Just from my own personal experience and friends that have their own story to tell, we all can relate in some form or fashion. Most women are so afraid or ashamed to bring up their feelings about their past and present that they don't even know how to put it in words. I feel this book gives those women a voice that can help them better understand their own emotions including myself. I look forward to having the opportunity to see what she writes next."

Ashley Pearson, Hotel Sales Manager

Endorsements, Reflections from Family and friends

"Elizabeth "Hope" Brown was truly an example to me. First Lady, mentor, friend, confidant & whatever the season called for. Reminding me of Paul, who knew his purpose, Esther who walked in her purpose, & John who showed love. Paul was all things to those who needed him, and Elizabeth becomes the same in a healthy Christ-like manner. For me she's always encouraging me to grow, breaking shells, and being all I can be! I love the way the book is so well written, that I can relate in one way or another to each character. Every character became alive to me. I believe this book goes well above and beyond its intended purpose. It truly pricks your brain about yourself and perhaps even the women in your life that helped shape you, and who you've become. It gives you the urge to self-evaluate to make sure you are the "true you." That is, who God purposed before you were born. "

Minister Shavonne Williams, Physician Assistant, Prayer Partner

"Having known Hope for over 20 years and never having heard the word quit come out of her mouth, I have no doubt that her new legacy for now and the future will be God inspired and full of love. Hope will prayerfully seek the words she needs to inspire and let women know their hearts need not be bound with God guiding their way. Always my friend with love from Granny CC."

C.C Wray, Retired Truck Driver, School Bus Driver

"7th Day is a thought provoking novel that causes you to consider the many paths life can take. As I read about each character, I am reminded of God's unfailing love for us in spite of what we've done or where we've been. I am confident that when each of these women wholeheartedly present their lives and circumstances to the living God, they will never be the same."

Gwendolyn Campbell, M.A. CCC-SLP, Childhood friend and sister in Christ

Endorsements, Reflections from Family and friends

"Exhilarating! Captivating! "And on the 7th Day...She Rests" is a work of art. It captures the thoughts and emotions of so many women. Situations from all walks of life are put to pen for all the world to see, hear with the minds ears, and feel with all your being. Every page drips with some part of each of us. This writing takes you to the uttermost depths of your soul. Elizabeth Brown brought to the surface emotions that have been buried for years. This book will compel you to re-examine your past and prepare you for your future."

Beverly M. Davis, Pastor's wife, Friend

"I think you're on to something great!"

Dr. Devon Eldridge, Psychologist

Table of Contents

Preface

This book is a creative fictional work. It is not an attempt to bash, insinuate or condemn any one person, nor groups of persons that may be able to relate to some of its content. Its intended purpose is to entertain, empower and inspire those reading it. Persons reading it should be enlightened, vicariously able to explore womanhood, and hear a voice given to those that have at times felt they had no sense of empowerment for themselves. It also gives a listening ear to the people that love them, and trying to better understand them. It's a collection of transparent stories with very practical events instigating awareness, healing, and hope. Everyone can relate to this book, as either a woman or as someone who knows one.

...And on the 7th Day, She Rests...

Introduction

I still remember writing my first novel. I was in the sixth grade. The cover was made out of a cardboard box, covered in construction paper, bonded with staples, white paste glue, with stick figure illustrations colored by crayons.

Over the years I've drafted many novels, of all genres, in my head yet they never made it to the pen and paper stage. The past three years I personally had to purge and be completely transparent with myself so that I could clear my mind to create the characters in this book.

For those of you that have received my email blogs, and followed me on social media, yes there has been a method to the madness. I've learned God truly does things in His own time, in His own way. Sometimes He has to shake things up, to get the best out of us. In being transparent within myself, it allowed me to be courageous in my own creative work. I really appreciate all of the likes, comments and feedback that I've received on my pages. It helped trigger and release my creative flow.

...And on the 7th Day, She Rests..., is an introductory bio-sketch of the lives of 5 women and a teenage girl. They are given a platform to tell their stories.

This book gives a reflective look of some of the things they've already experienced. We get a glimpse of non-discriminatory scenarios that any of us could find ourselves in. We see successful ways they've practiced avoidance, functioned through depression, practiced denial, and lived through the driving forces that helped get them to survive their pasts.

Throughout this book they are reconsidering paths for their future. It will conclude at the point that they are finally able to make practical connections as to why they have found themselves stagnant, experiencing merry go round results, and facing the true realities of their current situations. They each realize there's a need to change paths for a different future.

Introduction

Following this collection of reflections from each of their journeys thus far, we'll explore individually how each of them used their past experiences as a platform, to identify the real root of their problems and to empower their future. We will see the progress of their lives over the next decade. As this concludes, they are at the point that they've realized a need to surrender the life they know, relinquish the need to control or deny it, and get some much needed rest in the moment.

The number seven is used throughout the book as a moment of completion. A completion of what was, and the beginning of what will be.

Through their transparency you will laugh, cry, rejoice, and encourage them in the spirit to get some rest, and hold on just a little while longer while daring to become all that they were designed and created to be.

This novel can be used as a resource and icebreaker to reference topics that can be uncomfortable. It can also be used in book clubs, empowerment workshops, formal and informal teaching environments. Ultimately it can be read during personal leisure time to encourage others to tell their own story.

Chapter One

Darlene

I know that I am white. I don't need his mom, sisters, cousins, high school classmates and friends to keep referring to me as his "white wife." If I referred to them as his black momma, sister, cousin, classmate or friends, then I'd be a racist. I love my husband, and our life is tough enough with just the two of us trying to get along with the day to day matters of life.

I know it's hard for him to love me with my emotional issues, yet he loves me anyhow. I believe sometimes he feels as if he has to over compensate because of their lack of acceptance of me. It is to a point that no matter what I try, I'm still not good enough for him to them and to myself.

I've grown up in church all of my life. I graduated cum laude in under grad and from a prestigious pharmaceutical school. I never imagined sitting in an NA meeting telling strangers about my lack of ability to handle the problems in my life. I lost my job and licensure. I had an option to go to drug court or go to jail. Drug court seemed like the only rational option to me. I wasn't a junkie, I just got caught up in the moment. I don't belong in either one.

There was a time that I believed that if I could win his mom over, then the rest of his family and friends would naturally acquiesce to me, as it is evident she sets the tone in the atmosphere. When his oldest sibling passed away, I was the first one at the hospital. I spent every day and night with his mom for 2 weeks, cleaning the house before family and friends arrived for the services. I even pedicured her feet to help her relax. I cooked meals daily so that she'd have something on her stomach, facilitated phone calls, and helped with the funeral arrangements. After the burial, when all of the family and friends that gathered had returned to their lives, it seems like all she remembered was the fact that I was still white. I don't even recall her ever saying thank you, nor mentioning to anyone, that when no one else was there, I was still there. Not that I was doing it for credit or recognition. I didn't think much of it as I was doing the things I had done. It wasn't apparent to me that I had overstayed my welcome until she finally spoke directly to me in that familiar evil spirited voice, "when do you plan to take your white tail home?"

I was in the middle of washing dishes with my back turned to her while she laid on the couch that her now deceased child so frequently slept on. I just stood there frozen. She hadn't said much to me while I had been there, if anything. As I think back on it now, I have to consciously remove the idea that I think she was basking in idea of me attending to her as a servant, rather than appreciating it for what it was.

I dare not imagine how she may have felt having to bury her child. The closest I can relate to losing a loved one was when my mother died and how difficult it was for me as a teenage girl. Now as a mother my heart was heavy for her, and I felt inclined to do some of the day to day things that may seem minor in essence, but can be tedious in their execution when maintaining a household. She didn't see it that way. All she seemed to see was an opportunity to have hierarchy on me. She once said her son defied her when he married me. It's still evident she felt as if I had taken a role from her when marrying her son.

My husband and I have a daughter and son together and I guess I was hoping our children would wedge some of the tension and create a common bond. Our daughter was born first, looking just like her grandmother, only with a lighter complexion. The day she was born she herself admitted the physical similarities, despite the fact that she had told everyone that would listen that I was already pregnant when I met her son, and the baby was not his.

We married shortly after her birth and became pregnant with our son four years later. Marriage is rough, and our first four years was the epitome of everything you shouldn't say or do once you say I do. She was of no help. She always told her son our marriage wouldn't work, and was clear to her son that the door to her house was always open for him. She told me the day before our wedding that there was only one thing a woman could do for her son that she couldn't do. After a while that statement even became suspect.

When I was finally to the point of agreeing with her that our marriage wouldn't work, I found out I was pregnant with our second child. After I told him, the first thing he asked was that I not have an abortion. Though he never admitted there were problems in our marriage, it was shocking to me that he would think that I would consider aborting a child conceived by my husband.

My son was also born looking like a boy version of our daughter, and the twin of his father. Again my mother –in-law came to the hospital to give what seemed like another inspection to verify if whether or not her son was actually the father, and her grandchild. This time she grimaced and said that she didn't believe he could have any children. The reason why she thought her son couldn't have kids was never explained, nor did I dare to ask.

I was on bed rest with both of our kids during pregnancy and I still don't understand why. I developed issues with my gall bladder and was prescribed pain pills. Once I was discharged and returned to work the opiates helped me get through the day. My primary care physician refused to give me another prescription. Instead of going through the hassle, I just continued to go to different emergency rooms using alias in the area to get a few pills to get me through another day or two. They never prescribed enough to get me through the week. The time it took to sit in emergency room was ridiculous. I would leave work early so my husband wouldn't find out, and it worked until I started picking up our kids late from afterschool care.

Truly, our marriage wasn't perfect by any sense of the word, yet how could she not look at her grandchildren and feel a need for some sense of family kinsmanship and love? Naive would be the term best used to describe my belief in the hope that the love of her grandchildren would somehow supersede the hate and jealousy she had towards me as her daughter-in-law.

Instead, it only seemed to increase the tension and the idea that I had one upped her for the control and attention of her son. It almost seemed incestuous, as if she and I were in competition for the same man in an intimate relationship, and I was winning in her mind. Nothing I did was right in her eyes, and she was very verbal in the ears of her son to let him know of her disapproval of me.

I'm in love with a man, who's in love with me. Not because he's black, or because I'm white, but because we both love God and we are educated, consensual adults attracted to each other's ideologies and life goals. It's been 12 years now and a struggle for each one of us to die off to self and the things that hinder us from freely loving each other.

It seems that there has been no progress, no hope, and no idea where the time has gone, with no idea of what to do with the time that is left.

Most days I wake up with an ache in my back, a throb in my head, and heavy pounding in my heart. I wake up in the middle of the night from an apparent dream that disturbed my sleep that I can't recall or connect the events. I used to take two generic pain pills before I got out of bed to numb any feelings of anything until they no longer seemed to work. I found myself sipping wine in the evenings until bedtime just to relax and calm down before getting ready for another day. I've gained weight and I blame it on baby weight from both pregnancies even though my kids are both well into school age. One day at the pharmacy I slipped one of the opiates to the side while filling a prescription for a patient. Before I knew it, I was slipping one per patient refill daily until I was caught on camera.

As a pharmacist it became too convenient and easy to slide one extra pill to the side while filling a patient's scripts that contained opiates until the day I was caught. That day turned my entire world around. I've learned the judge sees the person addicted to prescription pills the same way he sees the homeless crack head, and closet alcoholic. The idea of being in the penitentiary system, and the humiliation of being in the court room was overbearing. I couldn't help but notice there were more white women than any other race in drug court. I know there has to be a reason for that. Do people really prefer to go to jail than do community service? Do people really prefer jail over sitting in narcotics anonymous meetings? Do people prefer jail to sitting down with a therapist and talking about learning how to better manage their behavior? From what I've observed, jail has yet to prove to be a place of rehabilitation and the reason so many people recidivate. It's almost an inevitable process once you're in the system. It will take 7 weeks for me to finish this program, and then it will be as if it never happened. I can get my license renewed, again be eligible for employment in my career, and not be considered a felon. In the meantime, we can live off of my husband's income and part of our savings.

All I've ever wanted is to feel love, give love, and receive love. I was a teenage caregiver for my mother before she passed away. There were so many unanswered questions that went to the grave with her, along with the love I never received from her.

Why did she never tell me she loved me? Why did she never hug me? Why didn't she come to any of my extracurricular activities at my school? Why were none of my gifts, friends, or compliments ever good enough for her?

They said she died of some type of disease that causes different brain disorders. I can't recall all of what the doctors were saying. I was young, and my grandmother still doesn't talk about it. It all seemed unreal watching her body change and how she would forget the simplest things and lash out on me when she couldn't remember. My education would suggest she suffered from dementia. My emotions believe she died of a broken heart from a man I never knew, with the love I never received.

Chapter Two

Theophilia

My sexual orientation is human. It doesn't matter at this point if it's a man or woman. I enjoy human companionship and contact. With all of the different LGBTQ, L,M,N,O,P movements, and questionnaires about how I identify, I've decided to create a box called "human." I knew I was sinking into a dark place of loneliness, when I found myself touching myself to the point of release and shame. Weeping in my own wet mess, trying to figure out what I had done so wrong to be in this predicament.

This was not the plan. Me of all people in line paying with a card issued to get free food for my kids and I. I didn't grow up on assistance. My mom was a single parent that worked overtime so that my siblings and I always had. As for our dads, out of sight, out of mind. They were different men with the same non-existent relationship with each one of us. The conversations about dads just never really came up. Most of the kids in our neighborhood didn't have a dad in the home, and the ones that did were either beating their wives, cheating on their wives, or coming home to their wives when they felt like it. Seemed to me like we had it better than them.

I guess the downside of all that work our moms put in was a lot of unsupervised idle time. They say it takes a village, and it was a village of us growing up together. Most of time we had fun playing and doing what most kids do. Before the creation of video games, we played make shift, innocent childlike games, which were created from rocks, tree branches, articles we found in the fields, with rules that we made up as we went. Once those made up games got boring we'd make changes. As adolescence kicked in, we made even more changes. Hide and go seek became hide and go get it. We began to identify the difference in each other, and now it's the boys against the girls and whichever boy caught you, he got to feel up on you in inappropriate ways. Then of course there was truth or dare. We took truth or dare to a whole new level the more we grew into our pre-teen stages and the curves, bumps, and puberty hairs began to appear on our bodies. There was less truth and more dares usually pertaining to someone showing, touching, feeling, or kissing body parts that momma and grandma said only fast girls allowed themselves to be touched in or you'd be going straight to hell.

Nowadays they call it molestation. So consider us all molested because everyone participated in one way or another, or you didn't get to play anything else. I guess it was molestation those days too, no one ever talked about it. Especially when something was done that you knew you should be ashamed of, but was more ashamed because it felt good to you and you looked forward to the next time you played. Sometimes, it seemed to cross the lines from the time we played before and you weren't comfortable with it, but you didn't know how to say no, because you went along in secret the last time. The exploration of our sexuality escalated and, instead of feeling good, I felt violated and ashamed.

I can't remember ever having the birds and the bees conversation or being told when it was o.k. to enjoy being intimate, how to date a boy without having sex, or how to please my husband or wife when I got married. In our community some things were just observed and left to your own interpretation to figure out as you experimented along the way.

Now, I'm a mom of three children. A daughter and two sons. My daughter is very helpful with her brothers. There's no love lost by any of their dads because there was no love there to start. I don't trust men. I think they're all perverts with only one thing on their minds when it comes to women. My mom used to always say she was fertile so be careful. It never really hit me what she meant until every man that breathed on me in between the women I was intimate with, fertilized an egg before they withdrew from me.

The one man that I did trust and love scared me so much I ran away from him. We also made a baby but she's his. We met in high school before I dropped out. He was so fine. An athlete with good grades. Both of his parents went to college and expected him to go too. Our neighborhood wasn't the greatest, but I was always smart. I was a teacher's pet, and prided myself on being the best in all subjects. My teacher asked my mom if I could test for a special high school. At first I said no because I wasn't retarded. Then she explained "special" meant it was for kids that learned faster. After taking the test and passing, I was bussed to the special school where we met. I loved it. For the first time, I felt like I was around other people that understood me and thought like me.

My test scores placed me in the accelerated math class. There were more boys than girls in that class, and for the first time I was confused. The teacher was going so fast and talking about how we should already know this stuff from last year. My school didn't teach that stuff in 8th grade. I made a C on the first test. My teacher suggested I get a good partner for the group assignment to bring up my grade. That's when he picked me. I was surprised. We never talked in class or outside of class. At first, I thought it was a joke and he was up to something.

We finished our project and got an A. It brought my grade up to a low B. After that, we worked together on our homework assignments. My overall grade came up to a high B. I turned in an extra credit project and then we took our first semester finals. I finished the first semester with an A-, then I kissed him.

He didn't see it coming. It seemed like the natural thing to do. After Christmas break, our afterschool tutoring became sneaking around campus to find blind spots to have sex in. We figured out the school grounds had a lot of spots in between the bleachers, in the softball dug outs, or behind the gym. I'd have to walk home, getting there after dark, lying to my mom about the reasons I had to stay after school and miss the bus. We did our homework. We were both smart and by the time I learned the system, I really didn't need his help anymore; I just wanted to stay after school to see him.

I got all A's and 1 B that year. I'm still convinced my science teacher didn't like me. I refused to dissect a dead animal so I lost points on my labs. Even with the B, I was proud of my grades, and looking forward to getting all A's my 10th grade year.

I knew I wouldn't see him over the summer. We lived in different neighborhoods, and I didn't have permission to have company from boys. I was hoping he wouldn't start liking someone else. He promised me he wouldn't and on the last day of school he gave me a teddy bear and some candy with a card signed "I love you." I didn't know what to say or do. My bus pulled up and I said, "Ok, bye."

Over the summer I didn't feel like doing anything. All I did was sleep, eat, and gain weight. By the time school started back everybody made it a point to mention I looked like I gained weight. I could still wear most of my clothes. I've always liked baggy clothes. They weren't fitting baggy anymore. Those days people called me a tomboy. I liked boys; I just didn't like to dress like a girl. That whole semester I kept gaining weight and sleeping in class. I was just tired.

Most days I rode the bus home because I didn't feel like staying after school. He kept asking me what did he do wrong, and if I was seeing somebody else. I didn't know how to explain to him he had done nothing wrong, I just felt different. My grades weren't what I hoped they'd be. Three A's, three B's, and that was with very little studying. I didn't know what was wrong, I was just glad that I made it to winter break and could get some more sleep. Then, one day I woke up in pain. I got up, moved around some, and then laid back down to watch T.V. most of the morning. By lunch time, that pain pill I took had worn off and this time it felt like someone was stabbing me in the stomach with a knife, and the knife was coming out of my butt. I drug myself to the bathroom and saw what seemed to be all of the blood in my body coming down my legs. I screamed for my momma over and over again until I blacked out. I woke up in the hospital to learn I had given birth to a baby girl.

When I opened my eyes, I could see the look of exhaustion and confusion on my mother's face. The room was silent for a while after I opened my eyes. Someone called the nurse in, and she explained to me what was going on. I didn't say a word for a whole week. They discharged us to go home and I still didn't say a word. When the social worker came to visit, I finally told her what happened and who the father was.

Long story short, his parents received DNA confirmation that they were grandparents and agreed to raise the baby. I haven't seen her since. I can't. I've never been the same.

Every other boy or man I've known since then seemed to either use women, lie to women, or treat women in a way that I always knew if they treated me in the same manner, my reaction would result in me going to jail. Getting emotionally attached was not an option.

I found myself fond of having sex, yet not vulnerable to the emotions that came with it. I've been with both men and women and have found both experiences physically gratifying.

I've never really considered myself in a relationship with a woman, but have called a couple of my male companions my boyfriend. My last boyfriend made me so uncomfortable around my daughter. While others tell me he's so good with my kids, and would make a great step dad, all I'm thinking is that's a little too comfortable for me. I'm guessing my childhood may have something to do with it.

In addition to all of the inappropriate games we played together as children, there were always those family rumors about the perverted uncles, and boy cousins that spent the night, and sometimes even siblings that were left alone while the parents were away. As a little girl growing up hearing those things from siblings and cousins, you become very guarded around those uncles that always compliment how pretty you are, and love you to kiss them on the cheek, or sit on their laps when, all of a sudden, what once felt like a cushion begins to feel like a knot rising in the center of your butt.

I'm supposed to be folding all this laundry, and some kind of way I've drifted off deep in thought. It's been at least 7 years since I thought about any of those things. If I have to listen to that singing dinosaur one more time I'm going to snap. But it works. It worked for the first 2, why reinvent the wheel. Whoever said being an at home mom was easy has never done it? If I hear one more person say "all you do is" they'll catch a back hand from me. I consider myself a domesticated engineer. Sounds more intriguing than an at home mom, and it still isn't descriptive of all that I do.

I'm not sure when the plan shifted from being a college graduate, corporate executive, power driven entrepreneur, but now it seems to be the aspiring dreams of a person I once knew. I can't change events of the past but I do realize I need to learn how to continue to live a productive life despite the things that have happened. I've had some experiences that I don't really know how to move on from. I think a lot of my decision making comes from being touched in an inappropriate way as a child. Not once or twice but several times by persons close to me that I loved and trusted as a neighbor, uncle, and childhood friend. After a while, I just started to pretend like none of these things happened. The memories I just couldn't forget, I decided to consider them normal and ok. It was just a part of growing up. No one else that I grew up with said any of the games we played or rumors we heard bothered them. Why am I the only one feeling guilty now? I'm too old and should be over it anyways. We're grown now, so why am I the only one still holding on to stuff that doesn't even matter anymore? I probably just made it up in my mind anyways. I've always been told I think too much and ask too many questions. I was looking through old photo albums one day and thought we looked like pretty happy kids. I'm 29 years old now, but why do I feel like I'm 92 instead? With all of the cigarettes I smoke, I'm surprised I can still breathe.

Sometimes I want to ask about my dad's side of the family. Now with all of the online resources I really can do it without asking my mom much at all. She told me who he was. Showed me a picture and everything, it just didn't connect. It was like looking at a stock photo in a brand new picture frame. I have this image of meeting him in person one day and then maybe I'll feel something different about him, and maybe even myself.

I said I wasn't going to be like my mom and have kids with different daddies and ended up with more than she had. What I did get from her is that I don't talk to any of their fathers. I don't know where 2 of them are and I'm not looking. I know one man is married and has a happy life with his wife and kids. He is more than happy that I do not disturb it.

Most people that meet me wouldn't believe my story. I still speak with an extended vocabulary, raise my kids as if all is well, encourage them to read and participate in extracurricular activities, and interact with a diverse group of people. We discuss the positive and negative things in life and I am very selective about who I let them go around. There is no spending the night anywhere and my daughter is not required to do any kissing, hugging, or sitting on the laps of anybody, related or not. I am verbal with her about that, and I make no apologies to anyone about the way I raise my kids.

I've made some mistakes. I've experimented with heavy drugs and it consumed me quickly. About 7 years ago, my high school sweetheart came looking for me. I never really recovered after that first devastating experience of having a child. I just didn't want to feel anymore. I remember seeing him, and hearing him say he didn't mind that I had a child with another man and he wanted to help me get sober and raise our daughter and my new daughter together, both as his own. I was too ashamed. He was a college graduate and said our daughter was doing well. He still loved me like the prince loved the step-daughter. I remember when he asked me to the prom in the school newspaper. I was so embarrassed yet flattered at the same time. He said he loved me so much that it scared me. He still looked at me in admiration as if I was edible. It made me squirm.

I never told him about the games we played in my neighborhood. I always felt like if I told him the truth he would look at me different and realize I was dirty and unlovable. When he touched me it really felt different. Like I was special. The best thing he could have done is let me go. After he finished talking, I told him our daughter was his daughter, and to leave me alone. Then I told him that I never wanted to see him or her again. I got sober on my own after that. Every now and then I smoke weed, and will drink a little something to keep me calm in the moments I just want to snap. Sometimes I still just think too hard and I'm afraid I'm going to completely lose my mind because of thoughts I can't seem to forget.

Then what'll happen to my kids? I'm all that they have by choice and circumstance.

It's just me and my three now. I call us the Fab Four and I'm determined they will have a better life than mine. I stay on them. They are great students, with polished manners. Though people may criticize me for receiving government assistance, I take it all in stride. Pride was lost after the first birth and all I can do about it is be there for my children that are still with me. I've had jobs with many hours and little pay and something always seemed to happen to my kids in my absence. I can't focus at work, too afraid of what all can go wrong while I'm away. So this is what it is for now.

They're changing the rules and have already cut some of my benefits. I have to go around to the different food pantries to keep groceries until the end of the month. I'm going to have to do something before my benefits are completely cut off. What that something is, I've yet to figure out.

Chapter Three

Olivia

"If a man ever hit me, I am going to jail." "I'll never let a man treat me like a pet and stay for love." "Ain't that much love in the world?" I guess it is... The doctors just walked out of the room asking if had I been hit or physically harmed in any way since this pregnancy and my answer was no. I lied. My husband was standing right there when they asked me. They even asked me if I wanted him to leave the room. I was too afraid to say yes, and too embarrassed by the idea that they may have picked up on something to warrant the question. It was easier for me to lie while he was standing there.

I've had several miscarriages and I don't know if I will or if I want to make it through this pregnancy. I want kids, but not his. They've been monitoring me for seven hours to make sure everything is ok. No everything is not ok. I hate my husband. This pregnancy is another result of being raped by my husband. I can't stand to look at my husband. I can't stand the smell of my husband. I can't stand to lie in bed next to my husband. That is how I really think about my husband. So why are we still together? Good question. It's like an addiction without a substance. I deal with women escaping domestic violence situations everyday on my job. As their case manager, I encourage them to not deal with this same issue yet everything I tell them, it is what I'm really telling myself.

This truly is a different world than what I grew up around. My dad never hit my mom or even gave the impression he wanted to. They say girls marry guys that remind them of their fathers. How did I end up marrying a man that has a problem with keeping his hands to himself? Not just him, but all of the men in his family seem to have this problem. They thrive off of drama, and peace is a foreign concept. It's a well-hidden family norm that people outside of the family would never catch on to. In public, they are the nicest, with their best manners, and eager to help and please anyone in need of assistance. Behind closed doors, a totally different person comes out. A mad person. A hurt person. An evil person with a vengeance against women. It's like they get consumed in the moment of their frustration and no longer in control of what happens next.

Every week, one of us wives are hiding in a closet, threatening to leave, struggling to hold on, and fulfilling our role in keeping up the misguided reputation of the family while suffering in silence. I've never told anyone in my family about this side of the relationship and living in different states makes it that much easier to hide. Even with the distance, sometimes I think my mom can tell something is off over the phone. I always knew if I made one call, someone would end up dead or in jail.

I don't understand how I didn't see this. I liked the way he spoke his mind and didn't hold things back. Sometimes his jokes went too far and felt like put downs but he'd apologize if I brought it to his attention. He told me he didn't have a lot of patience so I was always on time for things. He and his siblings would argue but I never once had a vibe or saw a sign while we were dating that he would have a short temper towards me. He was so romantic and charming to everyone around us. Before he asked me to marry him, everyone we came across was always telling me to make sure I didn't let him get away. "He's a keeper" they would say. I guess if something is too good to be true, it probably is a lie.

My family was charmed by him as well or should I say most of them. They didn't realize he wasn't as good of a man as he seemed. I should have caught the hint when his own momma said that he didn't have nothing, and my daddy should have met him at the door with a shot gun. He didn't have a shot gun, but when I introduced him to my daddy, the first question he asked him was "where his people from?" I was so embarrassed. After less than a 10 minute Q & A session, my daddy was less than impressed with him and called him a gigolo. I should have never told him what his mom said about the shot gun, because after that he called his momma crazy. Saying, "Who would say something like that about their own child they raised if it weren't true?" He told me "he is a user and it was just a matter of time before he used up everything I had." I thought my daddy was just being over protective of his little girl.

My daddy financially cut me off at that point telling me "he can pimp you, but he can't pimp me. You love him, I don't, so be willing to live the lifestyle that he can provide for you because I ain't taking care of no grown man." My daddy reneged a few times over the years because of his love for me. I'd leave him, ask my family for help and they would, then he'd call crying proclaiming he'd changed and I'd go right back to him. Finally, my daddy said enough is enough.

I left the first time he actually hit me. It was shortly after we married, over something I don't even recall. I moved back home and told my parents, I made a mistake marrying so quickly and I wasn't ready. Less than 24 hours later, he was there on my parent's porch crying with what seemed to be sincere tears of remorse. I had never seen a man cry like that before. I waited a week, then I moved back in. Then it happened again, and he cried again, and again, and again until his tears no longer moved me. I became numb inside. I used to believe he was sorry. I used to believe he wasn't going to do it anymore. I used to believe that the last time, really was the last time until he did it again.

I don't even know why anymore. At first he used to blame me for things that I could agree would make him upset. I've always been strong willed and freely expressed my opinion of things. People used to say my mouth was going to get me in trouble. I guess all the trouble has caught up with me because with him, I seem to stay in trouble. So I stopped doing certain things, started doing others, searching for the perfect way to fix myself so that he wouldn't have a reason to hit me anymore. I read magazines, redecorated the house in bright colors, joined groups with other married women and devoted my time on trying to figure out ways to make him happy, and keep the house at peace so that he wouldn't lose his temper.

The harder I tried, the more I changed, and the more he blamed me for the new reason he couldn't control his temper. He's destroyed so many things in the house until I will no longer decorate. Walls have been punched in, mirrors have been shattered, and pictures have been destroyed. We've even been in a car accident in midst of an argument that luckily no one was seriously hurt in. He usually leaves after a rage, and comes home to a clean house and make up sex filled with emotions, apologies, and promises to stop losing control of himself.

Now, my words have become less, and the house has become more and more silent. I stopped arguing. I stopped cleaning up the messes. You break it, you clean it up. Maybe after the glass he shattered cut him a few times he'd get it. The more I resist arguing, it only seems to make him even angrier. He doesn't drink, or do drugs, so I can't even blame it on that. It's to the point that he's starting to get mad over things that seem so minor and trivial I think to just get my attention.

I can't do this anymore. There's some real mental health issues going on. I've cried about it, I've prayed about it, and I finally said it out loud to him. He of course was again prompted into another rage indicating I was the one that needed some mental help because I didn't know how to be a good wife or treat a husband.

The pattern has been so consistent over the years I can almost predict his next flare up. I started keeping journals. Trying to figure out what I was doing so wrong to make him act this way. No one had ever accused me of making them feel this way. In fact, my reputation was the very opposite. After the first year of journaling, I started to see the patterns. I observed ways to prevent some of the outburst. I don't think he can help it. At least not on his own. He still won't admit he has a problem, and if I would just listen to him, and do as he says do, then none of this would be happening. There was a time when he had me convinced that that was true. Now whether it's true or not, I'm tired of living in a house made of egg shell floors.

My parents did not send me to college to meet a man that would beat on me. We fell in lust from day one. He acted like he couldn't get enough of me and I couldn't get enough of him. Before you knew it, he had moved into my apartment. We met on campus at the beginning of the semester. He said they had messed up his financial aid and he wasn't able to enroll but planned to get it straightened out by next semester. He didn't want to go all the way back home for one semester and was sleeping on the sofa of one of his old roommates.

I had moved off campus my sophomore year and was trying to finish up in four years to prepare for the real world on my own. My parents lived in a different state and they were no longer waiting up for me to be home by curfew. My parents have always trusted me. I've never given a reason not to. I can be responsible to a fault worried about what if's. I had a campus job tutoring and worked in the community. I had a one bedroom apartment because I don't have time for someone forgetting their half of the rent and I wouldn't have a place to stay. I don't like owing people, and after that first year of taking out a loan, I added up really quickly what I didn't want to owe when I graduated. I started working 2 jobs while going to school, while doing hair and typing papers for side money. I really didn't have much time to date, so when we ran into each other in the hall way it just seemed meant to be.

After he told me his situation, it seemed like a practical solution for him to move in with me. He was there all of the time and I could use his half of the rent towards my tuition. He said he was supposed to start a new job in a week, but they decided to go another way. Then he was going to find a different job to help out until he got back into school and received his financial aid. He never had a problem finding a job, it was keeping a job that was the problem. In his mind it seemed, his reason was always a good reason for why he'd quit. It didn't pay enough, the boss was disrespectful, he didn't like the hours, he needs time during the day to find something better, or he just didn't like it. When he did work the money never made it to the bill table. He either needed something for his car, a new outfit for his new job, or he invested into some scheme he and his friends were running to double their cash that didn't work nor did he get his money back. If he had .25 he spent .26 and borrowed a penny from me promising he'd pay me back.

He knows I'm smart and will figure out a way to make it. Once he moved in the utilities bills increased. He always wanted to eat out, and go out on a date that I needed to pay for until he got his next check. When the check would come he had to take care of something else, and something else, and something else.

We got married at the court house a month after he moved in. He said he didn't feel right just living together and he always knew when he met his wife he'd know she was the one. I was the one that he wanted to be his wife for the rest of his life. He had big dreams and plans once he graduated and was going to spoil me with the finest things for all the things that I had done for him.

At this point pride is why we are still together. I've always been competitive and can't remember not winning anything I tried, from the school spelling bee, to prom queen, to trying out for the cheerleading squad. I really wasn't into the girlie stuff and cliques, I just wanted to see if I'd make it.

The first time I ever failed a test in my school lifetime was the month he moved in. Everything moved so fast with me trying to help him get stabilized, that I wasn't prioritizing my time wisely to keep myself stable. I ended up quitting one of my jobs because I was just too tired to study. He never wanted people at our place, so I stopped doing hair and typing papers on the side. He kept saying if you just give me a month you won't regret staying with me. I promise you I'm going to be somebody one day and I'm going to make it all up to you. He insisted I'll never have to work again. I just listened but I never replied. I've never had a problem with working, and was raised to have my own. When we met, I was in college so I wondered where that idea came from.

His work checks were inconsistent and the bills started getting behind. One day I came home from class and the lights were cut off. He insisted he had already paid the bill with the cash I gave him and couldn't find the receipt. He said he'd call because he had already paid it. I told him I had already called and they said they hadn't received a payment. I wasn't prepared for the verbal assaults that came next. I was accused of calling him a liar, making assumptions and false accusations, and since I didn't believe him I could go ahead and figure it out myself.

The more questions I asked the more defensive he became and somehow, in a quick leap, he had both of his hands around my neck to shut me up. He immediately started to flood my face with kisses, hugging me, swearing he had never done anything like that before to a woman and would never do it again.

He had an insatiable appetite for sex. Being tired, having a headache, or having a period wasn't a deterrence or an option. When I would say no, he'd be enraged as if it was a personal offense towards his manhood. There were times that he'd literally tear my panties off thrusting himself inside of me just long enough to satiate his erection to prove he had authority of me, literally saying "don't ever tell me no again." Knowing the answer, I'd still lay there asking myself, "Can a husband rape his wife?" The next day, and sometimes the same day he'd turn around and be the most romantic, loving and unselfish partner yielding to please me several times before attempting to please himself.

This cycle of events has continued over the years. When times get rough, the physically tough guy leaves because of his mental and emotional weakness. Once I figured out a way to keep everything a float, he'd come back home with the reassurance to do his part next time.

I was watching TV one day and a televangelist was preaching about when you marry a person, you marry the whole family whether you know it or not. Before you say yes, be sure to go to a family reunion. You will know how well that person will handle life under pressure by the way their family interacts with each other. Confrontations always happen at the gatherings and whatever makes you uncomfortable then, won't change after you marry. As I reflect back on it now, I realize that was so true.

We didn't date long enough to get to a reunion. We actually never really dated at all. Because of his circumstance everything was done so quickly and in a hurry we introduced our families to each other along the way. He never did go back and finish school nor has he kept a job longer than a year since we've been married. He never finishes what he starts and everyone except him is to blame for that.

He was raised by a single mom that I was told by the whispers of others in the family that beat him to the point of abuse with anything within her reach in front of anyone present. They say, she called him everything but his name and assured him often that he reminded her of his no good daddy. They say, the daddy beat her just as bad until one day her older sister and husband that lived in another state finally came and got her. They say, he beat her to the point of death, and left her in emergency room alone to die. They say, his daddy rarely took her anywhere in the public, and the few times he did, he was so disrespectful it made everyone present uncomfortable. He was not quiet about the fact that he was ashamed of her and didn't want to be with her. He let everybody know love wasn't the reason they got married but the knowledge of her pregnancy was. They say, his abuse was his way of reminding her of that. That's what they say. My husband has yet to say anything about his parents to me.

If those things they say are true, my husband definitely got it honest and I am now suffering like his mom did. He once slapped me in the kitchen so hard my face twirled around and my ear hit the knob on the cabinet door and started bleeding from the inside. I had confronted him about a number a woman called me from that I didn't recognize asking for him. He never explained the call, and I haven't been able to hear properly out of that ear since.

I've never called the police on him. I've never wanted to see him in jail but I did want him to get some help. His mom always said if I ever had a problem with him to call her. She was no better than him with the excuses, justification of his behavior, or explaining to me what I was doing wrong as a wife to make him act this way.

Somewhere along the process I've been manipulated to believe I needed him more than he needed me, and didn't deserve any treatment better than I'm getting. I work with people that these types of things happen to, and somehow I've become one of them too. I've thought about a safe place that I can go to like the places I refer my clients. I need to be someplace he can't find me long enough for me to get myself mentally and emotionally together. Some place that I can focus on my strengths and self-worth. I need to be some place where I'm encouraged to stop believing everything he blames me for. He's figured out my weakness. I don't like feeling like a failure. I am afraid of how I'm going to make it on my own, especially now that my family has cut me off. I'm afraid to fail as a single parent. My dad has always been in my life. I'm afraid to admit the truth and reality that I've been making it on my on in my marriage, and carrying him along the way from the beginning.

I have forgiven him so many times that he no longer has respect for me. He's arrogant with it now, and he literally says to me he knows I'm going to take him back without even asking. Now he just shows back up at the door, and gives me that "is it safe to come in stare" and before I know it, I'm sometimes the one kissing and hugging on him like an addict feigning for another hit. It's hard to explain at this point. I started initiating sex for a sense of control and power before he could just take it from me like he used to in times past.

When he comes back, to me it proves I haven't failed as wife and I have another chance to get it right. We all have our vices and not all of them can be drank, snorted, injected, or smoked. I've become accustomed to the dysfunction and have taken it on as a challenge. The longer I'm in it, the more it becomes my norm. It seems like so much of me has been beat out of me, that I no longer recognize myself. He didn't win. I didn't break under pressure. I can take it.

I've become addicted to trying to fix him, while at same time allowing myself to be destroyed by him in the process.

Chapter Four

Apphia

Today is "I'm petty and I know it" day. I left my food on the table at the fast food restaurant just because I can. No I'm not letting every other person in line during the traffic jam, and yes I'm blocking the intersection to catch the light. I've been following all of the rules, being an organized planner all of my life. From the day I learned to write my name, I've been keeping a list of things to do by the day, and a bucket list of things to accomplish in my lifetime. I live by the calendar and have electronic spreadsheets to correlate my ideas.

It's starting to seem as if all of my planning has been in vain. It seems that all it has gotten me is being taken advantage of, burnout and used. I put up a good front and I'm quick to let people know I'm still feelin' myself. But as my mask loses its grip by the day, I'm learning, you can fool some people, some of the time, a lot of people most of the time, but you can never fool yourself. I was so busy working the plan that, in the end, I failed to let myself be human. I didn't have time. I was on the fast track of my 15 year life plan and being a part of any foolishness wasn't a part of it.

The one time I decided to take the risk, and do the carefree dance the way it seemed everybody else was doing, I never recovered from that broken leg. By the time I was a sophomore in college, I still hadn't had sex, tried alcohol, or even been high on anything but life. After everyone kept calling me the typical lame names and encouraging me to try some of this, some of that, and just a little more of this, at least once before I die. I gave in. In all of my planning, two things that were definite on my list. One is the day you're born, and the other is the day you'll die. A group of us hung out, and caravanned to several parties after the Homecoming game.

I really didn't think that I had tried enough of anything to wake up in the bed the next day with no memory of the night before. I was naked in bed with a guy I knew of but not enough to do something with that I had planned to wait for until marriage. I got up, sore between my legs and barely able to walk. My head was spinning, and I couldn't find all of my clothes including my underwear.

I left while he was still asleep. We saw each other on campus a few times after that, and didn't utter a word to each other or speak of that day. The next two months after that, when I went to the restroom and wiped I had a heavier discharge than normal, my panty liner would be soaked with an odor that even a fragranced douche couldn't get rid of. When my cycle came, I had painful abdominal pains I had never experienced before. I would itch in that area at the most inopportune times sometimes rubbing myself with a warm rag or dry towel until my skin was raw. I finally went to get a wellness check and was told I had a sexually transmitted infection and had had it for a while. So long in fact, that it would be difficult for me to carry a baby full term, if I was to ever get pregnant at all. I never wanted kids, but being told it may no longer be a choice of my own was a difficult concept for me to process. I only went off script one time. And one time was all it took to disempower me of one of my life choices.

That experience put me back on track to my original philosophy about life more rigid than I had been before. Anything not carefully thought out, and didn't make it to my list of things to do, will not be done. To include the type of men that I will date in my future.

It was a whole year before I even thought about going out with anyone again. I carefully thought of a list of things to look for in a man before going out again. If he broke one of the things on my list, I will not make exceptions to the rules or accept another date and I'm moving on to the next one. I was once told by a guy that I defect on a relationship before even giving it a real chance. I told him, I know what chances can do, and I wasn't willing to take another one.

My dad spoiled me growing up, and always told me never to depend on a man for anything. I grew up sitting next to him reading books and watching shows about history, animals, and stock investments. I've never owned a doll nor did I ask for one. I tried to babysit for money as a teenager over the summer my first year in high school. When school started back, I signed up for a typing class so that I could find a more suitable job for me the next time summer came around.

I created my list of male expectations to keep myself focused. I never thought I'd meet a man like me. I have never had a problem working hard and making my own money. By the end of my senior year in college I was well on my way to doing just that. Then I met him. I met the male version of me. He had his 15 year life plan set up on a spreadsheet like me. He didn't want any kids, like me. He wanted to make money and build an empire like me. After that one experience I was certain I was destined for greatness and purposed to be alone. We graduated from college and completed our graduate school programs and began investing and developing properties to store up for our retirement.

After 7 months of building and developing our dream house to live in together, I received a call from our realtor saying my fiancé' wanted to take his name off of the loan and asked if I wanted to continue the closing process in my own name. I had sufficient income, and better than good credit. I'm just confused. I started frantically looking through my list of things to do, confused by the call, repeatedly asking myself "What part of the plan was this?"

After seven years of dating, he said he wasn't ready to be married. Soon after, I learned he had bought a new house for himself, his former co-worker, and her two sons instead. The same former co-worker that many used to jokingly call his work wife. She became a young widow with two minor sons after her husband, a young healthy athletic man, died of a heart attack one day at the park while playing basketball. Her children were on the playground and she was walking the track. By the time the paramedics arrived, they pronounced him dead before ever leaving the court.

My ex-fiancé' tried to explain to me how they were just friends. He became a confidant to her, a mentor, role model, and even a recreational coach to her kids. He said spending time with them made him realize there was more to life than making money and building an empire. He continued to say she made him feel happy on the inside in a way that he couldn't explain, and her children made him feel appreciated and needed beyond what he'd ever thought of before.

As pride would have it I bought the house. That was the plan, and I followed through. Every now and then I'll over hear a conversation between our mutual friends about how beautiful their wedding was, a couple's vacation they all went on, and apparently she's pregnant again, which will make 4 kids all together.

His mom and I had a wonderful relationship. For years we had a standing brunch the same day of the week, often discussing plans about what was supposed to be our wedding day. For weeks after our break up, she would continue to call assuring me she will always love me, and our relationship didn't have to end because her son and I were no longer together. I made excuses for weeks to not go see her. What is there to talk about? Finally she stopped asking.

What did I miss? We had so much in common. We had great sex. It has never been so easy for me to talk to anyone. We used to work together on the plan. If the truth be told, if it wasn't for me he probably wouldn't have finished undergrad, and he definitely wouldn't have made it through grad school. I trained him, and it was during that time we became friends. What did I do wrong? When he was down on his luck and almost lost his car, did I not help him get a new one. When he got behind on his coursework and almost didn't pass a class, did I not tutor him in addition to getting my own work done?

I've been there for him. I've been consistent and always a woman of my word. Three months into his marriage, I couldn't believe he actually called me asking me to help him find some investors for a new project he was working on. Am I really supposed to help him continue to build his empire to enjoy with his new family?

I don't think I can do that. Right now I don't think I can do anything starting from getting out of bed every morning. Nothing seems to give me pleasure. I've tried eating my favorite foods, watching comedies on TV and at the movies, and I've exercised so much it looks like I'm sick. I have no appetite, being around people exhaust me, and for the first time since that night in college I thought about drinking or smoking something to make me feel motivated, inspired, or something other than what I am feeling now.

I'm mature enough to acknowledge my mistakes and accept the consequences of my actions. But I still don't know what I did wrong. I should feel fulfilled. Grateful about the things that I've accomplished. I've always been an over achiever and try to do things as close to perfect as possible. I go 110% for myself and others. I don't dummy down who I am to fit and people always know exactly where I stand on things. I volunteer my time and service. I give monetary donations to monthly causes. I treat people, the way I want to be treated.

People often ask me, "When will I start dating again?" I am dating. I am dating myself. Re-introducing myself to me. I'm intelligent, beautiful, financially stable, no kids, and I own my home. I stuck to the plan. Why am I not happy with it?

Chapter Five

Claire a.k.a "Chopper"

52 ways to die and counting... All it takes is one. There needs to be some kind of law for teenagers to take a stress test too. My granny is always talking about her nerves, blood pressure, arthritis, and all of her stress. Let me say something about mine. She will say something like "you ain't got no nerves." How does she figure that? I may not have what she has, but I have something and it doesn't feel right on the inside. Sometimes I think about doing stuff that's not cool. Stuff that can hurt me, and maybe even the people around me.

Just because I'm 14 doesn't mean I don't get stressed and depressed. One day, I slept all day and didn't even realize it. Sometimes I'm not happy and I don't even know why. Sometimes, you find out the truth about things, you prefer to be ignorant.

I've been on punishment for like 7 days for something the teacher said I did that I didn't do. If they would have asked me, I would have told them what I really did and would probably have to be on punishment for 7 more days. I feel like as soon as you get through the least amount of truth, which seems to be light, then you're surrounded by all of the darkness. But they're the grown-ups, and they know everything, so I'll let 'em. I'm actually glad they came when they did. This guy that I used to like, but still likes me, had just walked off.

What kind of person is born and never even meets their mom? I don't want anything from her. I just want to see her and see what she looks like. Maybe even hug her one time and tell her I forgive her and I'm not mad at her. Or maybe that I am mad at her. I'm still embarrassed about the time my teacher asked me if my mom wanted to be a room chaperone and I had to tell her I didn't have a mom. I guess I could've asked my granny.

Sometimes I wonder if I knew where my mom was I would feel better about myself. Usually it's the dad that leaves not the mom. My dad tries. I know he loves me but some things I just can't talk to him about it. I wonder how he would respond if I said things like "Hey dad, my flow's getting heavier this month can you go to the store and grab the larger tampons?" or "Hey dad, my left boob is a slightly different size from my right. Am I okay?" or maybe "Hey dad, this guy did something to my neck today ... is that like a kiss? Does it mean he likes me? Looks like it left a mark." Definitely not.

Maybe it's because of my dad and not me that I want to see her. I think he misses her and sometimes when he looks at me, thinks about her too. All I know about her is the little things I've heard when the family rumors starts murmuring. Usually it's with sarcasm at the family gatherings during the holidays and reunions. Anything that they perceive negative about me, of course I get it from my momma. My dad is the favorite grandson, son, nephew and cousin that always comes to the rescue of the damsel in distress pattern of women in our family.

Once upon a time I thought I was finally going to have something close to a real mom. I was going through an odd stage in my life adults call "puberty." I was feeling as odd as the word sounds to me. She used to come to our church and noticed some of the days I wasn't so happy. Some days were more obvious than others especially when I wasn't dressed in "church" clothes. Like some of the other women in the church, she started offering to buy me things more girlie, unlike the outfits my dad considered appropriate for his Princess. I don't mind people buying me stuff because I'm still going to tell my daddy the truth if I don't like them. Unlike the little girls that dressed like a baby doll, she convinced my daddy I was ready for my first pair of heels. She also would stop by on Saturday nights and help my daddy out by fixing up my hair and tying it up for the night. She'd bring homemade meals made from scratch, encourage me to keep my room clean, and sometimes would stay and watch our Saturday night family movie with us. A couple of times she even rode with us to church. There was this one time when she even helped me to convince my daddy to put Kool-Aid colors in my hair and we said it was for a science fair project. When she was around, we started to feel like I always imagined a real family should.

One day after church service the fairytale came to an end. When she first joined the church, she said her job moved her here. Come to find out, she had several warrants for her arrest in her home town for fraud, assault, contempt of court, failure to pay child support, and harassing her daughter's father's wife, who also claimed she tried to run her off the road. What! How can a woman with no kids owe child support? Turns out she had 5. From four different men, only because she had a set of twins. The way she rocked a bikini you would never know it. Not a stretch mark in sight. I guess it's true that not all women get a wormy tummy or she has a great plastic surgeon I'm going to look for when I get older.

Everybody in the congregation just sat there in stares. They arrested her in the church saying they had been looking for her for three years. Somebody recognized her on the church's social media page and that's how they found her. There was a lot of stares yet none like the one on my daddy's face. I've never seen that look of hurt and humiliation in his eyes before.

I felt like I was partly to blame. I've never allowed anyone to get that close to me before. I even shared with her my thoughts that at that time was 25 ways to die and wanting to meet my mom one day. She once wrote me a letter about how honored she was to be a mother figure in my life. I believe that is part of the reason my daddy let his guard down and started seriously dating her. I know he wanted to see me happy and he wasn't really sure how to do it. I wasn't his Little Princess anymore instantly healed when he'd blow kisses on my cheek and it made everything ok. There are some things I'm told that require a mother's touch that dads just don't have. I want to feel that touch too.

The other women that tried to get close to my daddy where much more obvious with their intentions, in a lot less time. They really just wanted my daddy. The closer they thought they were, the less attention they paid to me. At first it would be the little things like the way my daddy and I sit together on the couch and watch our Saturday movies. All of a sudden, they wanted to suggest we change seats, so they can straddle across him on the love seat where there's only room for two. Or they would start comparing stuff anytime he did something for me, they'd ask him to do it for them too.

For some, he couldn't even give me a compliment, without them asking him to duplicate the compliment but they would top it with an intimate kiss. The biggest thing they would do was stop wanting me to tag along. They would pout for him to spend more time with them away from me. If that didn't work they'd start knit picking everything I did, telling my daddy things he needed to watch about me, as if they were trying to turn him against me. There was this one time when one of them even accused me of stealing something from her that she gave me permission to borrow. If those women didn't hear anything else about my daddy they heard he put me over everything, and to get to him, they had to first get past me.

This time was so different. She was such a good liar. I've always had trust issues with women. Growing up without a mother it wasn't easy for me to believe she cared about me, but I did. As it turns out I was just a way to my daddy to her too.

We later learned after sitting through her trial process, that she had long history of manipulation, deception and lies. She continued to lie to my daddy throughout the process, accusing everyone of lying on her. All of her children were born under deceptive vices. The oldest was born after she collected sperm from a condom and had it artificially put in her some kind of way. The child's father was a military man that always used protection. When she became pregnant she blamed the condom for breaking. Once the baby didn't keep his attention towards her, she left the baby with her momma to pursue her next prey.

She had twins the second time. She told their father she had given birth to a child whose father had died in a car accident leaving her as in single mother trying to finish her college degree. She told him how she wept and cried before making her decision. She told him how she couldn't do it on her on, and finally made the decision to give her baby to a couple that could. He fell for her and her story. He asked her to marry him so that they could have many more babies together. Unexpectedly the child's father returned home from combat duty. He had hired a private detective to find her so he could serve her court orders asking for visitation of his child. By the time the truth came out, not only was she pregnant, but with twins. He fought for custody of his unborn twins and took them home with him at birth.

The fourth baby could have been on one of the many paternity talk shows famous for revealing the baby's father. The first person she blamed had a vasectomy after his divorce. The next three people tested were "not the father." The fifth person was open to the idea that it was possible, and the sixth one said not a chance. The seventh and final person turned out to be the father, a man that already had 20 kids and wasn't interested in adding to the squad. She left that baby with her mom too.

The last baby she had was with a married man whose wife couldn't have kids of their own. He was remorseful about their affair yet excited about the idea of being a father. His wife stood by her husband and she tried everything she could to break their bond to end their marriage. For less than a year, it was a chaotic attempt at co-parenting. She was always calling for something even when they had the baby. She threatened to kill the wife and even called him from the hospital once saying she tried to kill herself since she couldn't have him. They transferred her to the mental health facility from the emergency room. After that episode didn't persuade him to leave his wife, she decided she didn't want anything to do with the child and left him and his wife to raise the baby as their own. The biggest surprise was that her youngest child lived right here in the same city.

She couldn't even keep up with her own kids, what made her think that she would be able to keep up with me. Now she made me think even more of my mom, in the worst way. In the end I guess I felt better that I wasn't the only person she fooled. I don't think that it made my daddy feel any better. My granny said that's the closest he'd ever come to loving another woman since my mother turned him away. He hasn't been on a single date since. My daddy doesn't do well with being made a fool of. My granny said no one likes to be made a fool of especially a man. Maybe it's his pride. He asked me once what did I think about her being my step mom. I said "I think it's a great idea." I was excited about the idea of having a woman in the house, to talk to about boys, help me pick out a prom dress, and play in make up with. I wonder if he was planning to ask her to marry him.

I don't know what made me think of all that. There are too many people in the world for me to be talking to myself. Am I wrong? I need to be thinking about stuff other girls my age think about. Are there any girls who care more about their grades than boys, hair, and clothes? I'm to a point where I think I'm more concerned about my education than anybody else. It's storming outside. I'll tell my daddy I caught a cold and suggest that I stay home. I know he'll get super worried and keep asking me if I'm ok. He's always acting like he's guilty of something, and it always seems to me like it's because of my mom. Sometimes I want to say "Dad, I'm ok with not knowing who she is. You not bringing it up isn't making it any better."

My mother never gave me a name before she left the hospital, so my granny named me Claire. She said it means bright or clear. She said the day she brought me home, even with everything that was going on around me, she could see so much brightness in my eyes.

I named myself Chopper because I'm too fly! Yeah I know who my daddy is but who is there to tell me that he really is my father? Someone please tell me this man and I have the same nose! Chin? Eyes?! In third grade I did my black history report on a man with the last name X, simply because he didn't want a slave name. How do we know if any of our parents are our real parents? All we know is what they tell us. I don't want to claim a name that's not mine, or I don't know the full history and truth of it.

Just call me Chopper...

Chapter Six

Isabella

After 25 years of trying be who everybody says I should, verses who God created me to be, I've decided I'm done. I've tried to fit into the boxes, wear the suits, hats, speak the language, and follow church protocol. Everybody seems to know my role, but I can't seem to find any sound scriptural reference to confirm it or justify why it only applies to me.

My gender, who I'm married to, or the opinions of others, is not a valid resource to determine if rather or not I'm the person God has called as a vessel to undergird a ministry that He has joined together. I've read the word. I've researched the word. I've prayed for revelation about the word, and I've yet to find confirmation about how to be a good pastor's wife based on the vote of the people.

I knew when they asked about having another women's gala, that it would be the last time we celebrated something that biblically doesn't exist. I've been in the world and of the world. I've been places I shouldn't have been. I've said things I shouldn't have said. I've done things that I should not have done, with people I should not have even been around. When I put those things behind me, I left them there.

I married a preacher at his request. I never imagined myself as a preacher's wife. Nor even considered dating one. I guess I thought they had some kind of arranged marriages or something. 25 years later, I am still persuaded it was God, and God alone, that designed our marriage to be.

As times and trends have changed, so has our relationship and protocols in the church. More and more the ways of the world have become a part of our worship experience and it's becoming acceptable. I'm not speaking in judgment yet in fear of the ramifications for those of us that know better, yet choose to not do better. No matter what changes in this world, the God we serve stays the same.

When they asked me about the program for this appreciation event, I guess my response was not what they expected. Before I spoke a word, I began to pray. When I opened my eyes the clock had advanced seven minutes.

On the evening of, I said a speech. "And now, for the moment that we've all been waiting for...

Most of you thought you came here to celebrate me. But we're actually here to celebrate each of you and all of us. I believe that a man or woman deserves to receive honor when it is due, but our greatest reward comes from God at the end of our journey. I have had fun with planning this year's event. I knew tonight would be a special night for everyone. The only two things I requested of our chairperson was that I wanted to do the speaker presentation this year, and instead of an appreciation, I wanted to do a "Dinner with The First Lady." I have enjoyed all of the appreciation dinners in the past, however, I really have more of passion for women's workshops and fellowship rather than a kudos party for doing what the Lord has called me to do.

I remember when my husband and I first started in ministry together years ago. I immediately prayed and asked God what my role would be. His response to me was that my husband and children are my ministry right now, and over time that would change. Over the past 25 years they have been more than enough. Others have benefitted from my service to them, but my platform of the things I've done was inspired and motivated by the needs of the house.

Because of my gifts and the instigations and agitation of others, I've been tagged with unmerited titles of evangelist, prophetess, bishop, and apostle. People have gotten very loose with God's appointments. You have to be careful not to let others put something on you that God didn't call you to do. Those same persons will not be around to help you carry that burden, and neither will God.

It's just as important to not allow people to speak out of you what God has put in you. Don't deny your calling because they don't see it or agree with God's choice. I'm in no hurry to complete my journey here on earth, but when my time comes, and all of us have a time, my desire is for the eulogist to be able to say I truly was a woman that fought the best fight I could, finished what I started and kept the faith in doing so.

So Ladies, we are in dress rehearsal tonight. I know that I'm not the only one that God will reward. He will reward all of us that serve faithfully longing for His return, doing what God has called us to do. We're going to trade in these hats and crowns we're wearing tonight, and get the eternal reward at the end of our journey here in earth.

I'm known to point out the elephant in the room, so I will address and rebuke the fact that there may be a person in this room that came to be nosey or to have something to murmur about. My husband preached last week that when Jesus picked His disciples, He knew that one of them was of the devil and would betray him. When you're planning for God, you can't be naïve, yet expect these things. It's ok if you are here for that reason, because we already have your donation. It was gladly received and the caterer has been paid in full. But I warn everyone in my company, you may have come for one reason, but you will leave with what God intended for you to have.

Most people here know me, so I'm believing that everyone else in this room is here for Jesus. It's difficult for people to celebrate others. When you do things like this, it's always interesting and many times surprising who shows up, and who's absent.

As a married woman and Pastor's wife you figure things out real quick, especially when it comes to other women. You begin to notice things like, you stay in my husband's face, but you walk the perimeter of the sanctuary to avoid speaking to me. You try to bribe my kids with gifts to win my husband's favor, but you avoid eye contact with me. You bring a plate of food from home for Pastor, but we're a household of seven, and you're purposely trying to cause division. I told the women's group that meet monthly, if you send a cake or pie home for Pastor, do know, that my kids and I will be eating the cake or pie too, so please make enough with that in mind.

Then there's the ongoing emails, texts, calls, and verbal complaints about what I'm doing, not doing, and should be doing, wearing, not wearing. We won't even mention the debates about where I am supposed to sit. Do you not realize that when you tear a man down, put thoughts and suggestions in his mind to make him doubt, lack trust or make judgement against his wife, who's usually the stabilizer of the home, you're taking him away from his family which is his foundation? You may gain your selfish desire and momentary attention, but you and everyone else will lose the full essence of the God in him that God's people are depending on.

Now he is unstable as an employee, mentor, and no longer a sound preacher practicing what he preaches in the gospel. He may still preach it well from his mouth, yet people are doubting what he is saying, justifying their own bad behavior, using his decision making as a rebuttal saying "if the preacher did it, so can I."

His mind and spirit will constantly be unrested because they're trying to combat all of those spirits, while continuing to preach. If you're one of these type of women, please know that you're provoking them to function in a dysfunctional manner, and it's only a matter of time before they burn out.

The bible teaches us to pray for our leaders and their families so that you, and everyone around you can continue to effectively get what you need, and not what you want. If you know of any of these types of women, pray for them as well because they really don't know the full scope of what they doing. They are weak women, being used by the devil who doesn't know God's ultimate plan.

Even with all of the obvious attacks, I'm so grateful to God to continue to be used as a willing vessel.

Our theme is Royal Priesthood: I'm going to give you a personal example of how you can bless and curse the next generation at the same time. My birth wasn't so royal. As a matter of fact it was a pretty humiliating experience for my mom who was raped by her uncle shortly after he walked in on her losing her virginity to her first love.

My mom's uncle stayed in and out of jail. Every time he would get out, her mom would let him come stay with them saying he was her little brother and she couldn't let him be out on the streets. Right after he raped my mom, he told my grandmother about walking in on my mom and her boyfriend, yet never told the part about what he did after. When she found out she was pregnant, my grandmother sent her to live with her grandmother in another state. My mom wasn't sure if I belonged to her boyfriend or her uncle. When I was born she named me Isabella which means "pledged to God."

Growing up I've always known what my name meant but I never knew why. One day when I was a teenager my great uncle was in a bad accident and he needed a blood transfusion. Most of our family was tested to see if anyone was a match. When my results came back, I wasn't a match. I thought my mom was crying so hard because she was worried about her uncle. He died in the hospital. That's when my mother told me what she had never told anyone before about what he had done to her. For years I always thought my father was a hero that died trying to save someone else's life.

I learned in that moment to have hope in hopeless situations. It all seemed to come natural. I came across a scripture, that revealed that "I'm a Queen in God's eyes," and the reason I stay faithful to his word. I know I will inherit the fullness of the earth, and that's something to be glad about.

As I became a young adult, I lost focus. I've learned darkness can be a state of mind acted out by anything substandard to the lifestyle that God has meant for you to live. It could be a lack of education, debt, or unhealthy relationships. Some of us are hiding behind a mask. We are living in the shadows of others trying to be what makes others comfortable in our company, but afraid to be whom God has destined us to be. I've worked in places that only sinners go. It was persons who described themselves as a sinner that told me I didn't belong there.

I'm sure I'm not the only one that had a season or two in our lives that we took some time away from God. We grew up real quick once we were exposed to the unmentionables. The things that I was exposed to, in a short period of time, had me running back to God. Now I have an even greater testimony, a stronger relationship with God, and there's no turning back.

I will send out a disclaimer now that I will not be singing songs of independence from men, or leading women in a parade of burning bras. I'm am in no way suggesting we don't need a man. I'm encouraging you to first not to be ashamed of yourself especially of your past. It simply means you were stronger than whatever it was that you went through.

Some of us have internal wounds. They seem to hurt the most because it's harder to identify the source of your pain. It takes trial and error before you get an accurate diagnosis, and can begin to heal. The healing required can be interpreted in the physical and spiritual. God can heal all wounds.

The second thing I'm going to encourage you to do is to not be afraid of what God has called into your life and the changes or losses that may be a result of it. I don't believe the Lord will allow us to lose anything that He truly meant for us to have, no matter what the situation looks like. Sometimes we may even have to get away from our familiar surroundings to really see the difference in our maturity and physical growth. Had we stayed home, we may not have noticed a change as quickly.

Daring to be all that God has created you to be is a process. It will take discipline and sacrifice. As I was preparing this speech, I was battling in a tremendous spiritual warfare. Unlike times before, I've found myself not only not responding like I used to, but also not having the desire to respond like I used to. I've had a couple of slips along the way, but I've been much quicker to repent, overlook, or forgive depending on the situation, and continue to show kindness in spite of.

I have found myself continuing to pursue what I believe God would have me to. Before you can expect people to respect and admire you, you have to respect and admire yourself. You have to feel and treat yourself the way you want to be treated. Unfortunately, most people will treat you the way you allow yourself to be treated. Some of us think more lowly of ourselves than other people do, and no matter what they say, you won't believe it, because you don't believe in yourself.

Who do you blame for your lack of achievements or feelings of inadequacy? Is that the truth and do you use them as scapegoat for the way you feel about yourself? How long do you get to use them as the excuse for not proceeding forward? Before starting the process, ask yourself, do you admire the person you've become, and would you like to be like you when you grow up? What would you change?

I've had that Superwoman season of life trying to be all things, to all people, all at the same time. Knowing who to be, when to be, what to be, where to be, and why to be there comes from God. It also takes being equally yoked with spouses, friends, co-workers, and family members that understand what your current goals are. You will have to be patient with those closest to you. They may not understand, they may misinterpret, or misperceive your internal need to change. No matter what they say or do, you will have to trust God and know that it is Him working within and will touch the heart of those He needs to touch.

We've made it this far by faith Ladies. Take a moment to look around the room, smell the room, and think about what has been said thus far. How do you feel about the sacrifice you made to come today?

I was always taught to try to end on a positive note, so I will start with saying you are not called into substandard living. You shouldn't be using anything less than 100% of the potential God has placed in you. Don't be in the habit of only displaying the characteristics that make the people around you comfortable.

You are not called to be oppressed or depressed. If you only go to church when you are unhappy, there is a problem with your relationship with God. If your unhappiness only comes from the affairs, ministries and people at the church, there is problem with the relationship with the church and God. That is not God's intention. You should be enthusiastic about coming into God's house.

You were definitely not created to be abused physically, mentally, emotionally, spiritually, or financially. As women, we are strong creatures. We know how to be who we need to be, to get what we need done. We can become true chameleons to please others or manipulate them to get what we want, for the time, and task at hand.

We've taken in so much figurative trash that our garbage has started to overflow, and our attitudes about life stink. Some of us have yoked up in relationships with ungodly men and women that provoke ungodly behaviors. When this happens, we are dangerous, cancerous, and destructive to all that cross our paths, inappropriately using our strength, trying to do what God has already said is done.

We as a body, are going to have to get out of putting people in roles not assigned by God. Ask God, who are you supposed to be? Then surrender to God's will for your life. Stop trying to control what He's called in the life of others. Embrace His will with obedience and a positive attitude. Doing things for God with an alternative motive isn't going to get it. If in your mind, you're saying things like, "I'm doing this long enough to just get this, or to do that." Stop it. God knows your heart. Sometimes He'll even let you get what you think you were manipulating Him for, but when you get it, there's no gratification, and it doesn't feel like you thought it would feel, or be like you thought it would be.

I love being a wife, mother, Christian and active in the church. I didn't love the process to get to the point of standing before you today. I didn't love the sacrifices and unselfishness that was required to stand before you with confidence in speech. I didn't love the anger and frustrations that would arise in me when I felt impatient or incompetent while trying to do the things that I thought were right. Many times people that I helped responded with a spirit that lacked gratitude or appreciation. Other times, the people that benefitted directly from my service, failed to acknowledge it, or proceeded as if they did it on their own.

I have matured to a place to realize that all those thoughts, emotions, and feelings are valid. What's even more valid is remembering why I do what I do. I do it for God. His will, His way. I remembered God does things decent and in order, and only what I do for Him will last.

In daring to be what God has called you to be, you usually become someone that doesn't look like you envisioned yourself to be. Now, I can't see myself any other way." ~End of Speech~

Apparently that speech wasn't received the way it was intended. The next day, they had a called meeting at the church, prompted by the complaints of some of the wives of the church leaders in attendance. Someone raised a motion, then someone seconded the motion, and a unanimous vote was made. Within three days after the vote of the church members, I received a legal, certified letter in the mail stating I was no longer welcome on any of the properties of the church...

Chapter Seven

She Rests...

As the preacher stood in the pulpit, and simply said, "In the next 7 seconds I want ya'll to give God your best praise and watch the shift in the atmosphere. 7, 6, 5, 4, 3, 2, 1 ..."

Darlene

I'm not sure what just happened. I woke up this morning feeling like I needed to go somewhere, but where? Back to where I grew up being on this day every week. When I walked in it felt different. Different from the way I remembered feeling when I was a kid. When the pastor started the count down, I started to look down. I started thinking about the times I would hear the old people in the church say their hands looked new and oddly enough so did mine. Then I looked at my feet and they did too. Is this what they were talking about when they said if you have a change of heart, then things no longer look the same? Now my heart is burning, and everything within my bones, and I can't do anything about it. Everything in me is moving and shifting, shifting and moving, while at the same time staying in place. I want to say it hurts, I want to say it feels good, whatever it is, it definitely feels different. Different than I've felt in a long time. Different than I've ever felt before. I belong here. I've been here before. It's where I first learned the true identity of the one who first loved me...

Theophilia

I am not a performing artist, and I do not shout on cue. For the next seven seconds I'm going to give god exactly what god has given to me. Nothing. Nothing that I want to give him praise about anyways. I'm going to give him the same hell, bitterness, strife and the best of nothing that he gave me. If this was the best he had to offer, then why did he create me? I don't even know why I'm here today. It ain't Christmas, Easter, or Mother's Day. The only reason I come on those days are to let my kids outshine these church folks kids. You can't beat them to the church. They act like their kids are better than mine. Their kids are here all the time but don't know how to act in church. My kids know I don't play. And when it comes time to say their speeches, I make sure they get the longest one and they will not be reading from no paper. These women in here act so sanctified and holy, and they run behind the pastor and the church more than they run behind their own kids and the school house. Then they let the pastor play on their emotions by hollering on cue. I don't think so. I've read the bible too much for myself. I do imagine sometimes a day when people can just be real, get together and really have a good time in church. From what I see, most of these people are just running around hollering because it's a safe place to vent frustrations they can't control. I really just needed to get out of the house and stop thinking. I knew this would be a place where I would be around a lot of people. The temporary distractions would allow me a moment to just be, not thinking about what will happen tomorrow...

Olivia

After all I have been through I'm still alive. Every punch, every slap, every condescending word, and even being spit upon, I'm still alive. I just can't believe I'm still here for no reason. I just can't believe I've come this far, not to go any further. I laid in the hospital and thought, this time I was going to kill him. I really was at the place of homicide or suicide, because something had to give. I told one of the nurses indiscreetly what was really going on and she referred me to a secure home where they help women in similar situations as myself. I didn't tell my husband when I was ready to be discharged. When he left to go take a nap, someone I didn't know, but trusted more than I trusted myself, or what I might do if I went back home, came to get me. The home that they took me to, has a van they use to take the women housed there to worship if they choose. I'm glad I came to church today. I'm glad I came and was asked to give my God my best praise. I didn't know how I was going to get out of that situation. I didn't know when I was going to get out of that situation. But what I did know, is that I needed to get out of it. I have none of my personal belongings with me and it doesn't matter. I was asked before we left the hospital, what was I willing to give up to get myself out of that situation, my response was everything...

For the first time in my life I have no logistical plan of action or clue as to what to do next with my life. I've always had everything in my life perfectly planned out, but I didn't consider I might have issues. I've been sitting here, looking at this card and my phone as if it's going to magically dial itself. Someone recommended that I go speak to someone professional about my current mood shifts. I am a professional. I finally made the call and she said this is normally her day of worship but she must have picked up something in the sound of my voice and agreed to meet me at her office. I'm not sure if it's a comfort, or if it makes me uncomfortable that I just assumed a clinical minded person wouldn't embrace spiritual minded principals as well. If that's the case, I could've just went to church. We sat there quiet for some time, and finally she broke the silence and asked me a question with instructions not to answer before counting down starting at 7. By the time I got to 1, the floodgate of tears began to uncontrollably run from my eyes, down my face...

Claire a.k.a. "Chopper"

Why are preachers always telling people what to do? "Hug somebody," Look at somebody," and my most dreaded, "Tell your neighbor." My daddy be right up there in front co-signing like he is the hype man or something. I look around trying to understand why everyone is crying, running, and even waving their hands and saying amen. I don't get it, just like I don't get why my mother left me. I didn't tell my daddy I started reading my bible. I'm trying to read it in 365 days from cover to cover. I think I can do it if I divide the pages right.

Isabella

Lord I have told too many people about you not to give you praise. I'm sorry for my stubbornness Lord. I really have been struggling with my faith. I have been in the church, but the church hasn't been in me. I've been purposely trying to submit to my flesh to do unto others just as much hurt that has been done to me. It just isn't in me to treat them the same way. I have truly given them to You. If nothing else Lord, I thank you for keeping me in my right mind. Truly If You don't do anything else, You have already done exceedingly and abundantly above all that I have asked or even thought to ask of You to do. God I thank you for loving me, keeping me, forgiving me, and blessing me in spite of the things that I have done to myself. You truly are no shorter than your word. I pray that you continue to use me as a vessel in the lives of my household, and those around me, to lead and guide them in the way that You would have them to go, "Daring to be all that You have designed and purposed them to be" to Your Glory in ALL things...

It is the 7th day Ladies, now rest...

What is your story?

About the Author...

Elizabeth Hope Brown is a Social Worker, Non-Profit Organizer, Entrepreneur, and Speaker with over 20 years of community development experience serving in churches, communities, and schools. She started in grass roots organizations she grew up in as a child and immediately took on leadership roles.

Elizabeth describes her life as being filled with many events throughout the different seasons of her journey. Her home is decorated with medals, trophies, diplomas, and certificates of accomplishments from everyone. Her role in the process may not have always been visible to her family, yet to herself she admittedly pats herself on the back saying, "You did that!"

Elizabeth has been referred to as a daughter, sister, friend, classmate, niece, girlfriend, wife, auntie, student, employee, trainer, teacher, mentor, coach, at times the enemy, and now an author. She describes some events in her life as short lived sprints, while others seemed more like a decathlon. In her perception, she's placed in the gold, silver, and bronze on events, while failing to qualify in others. Today, she writes from a platform of observation and experience, unashamed, fully determined to be the greatest that she can be. "I've dared to be, and becoming more and more of the ME that I was designed, created, and purposed to be." Elizabeth Hope Brown

Today, Elizabeth is the founder of Lyzee's Hope, a platform dedicated to inspiring women and building healthy families. She loves to read and travel. Her life goals include visiting each of the United States, stamping all of the pages of her passport, and sprinting 400 meters with her daughter. Elizabeth is a graduate of Sacramento City College, Sacramento, CA, and Augusta University, Augusta, GA.

To contact or more information:

Est. Fourteen Forty-one

Post Office Box 16142

Augusta, Georgia 30919

fourteenfortyone2016@gmail.com

Chapter One Notes

Chapter Two Notes

Chapter Three Notes

Chapter Four Notes

Chapter Five Notes

Chapter Six Notes

Chapter Seven Notes

Made in the USA
Columbia, SC
05 September 2022